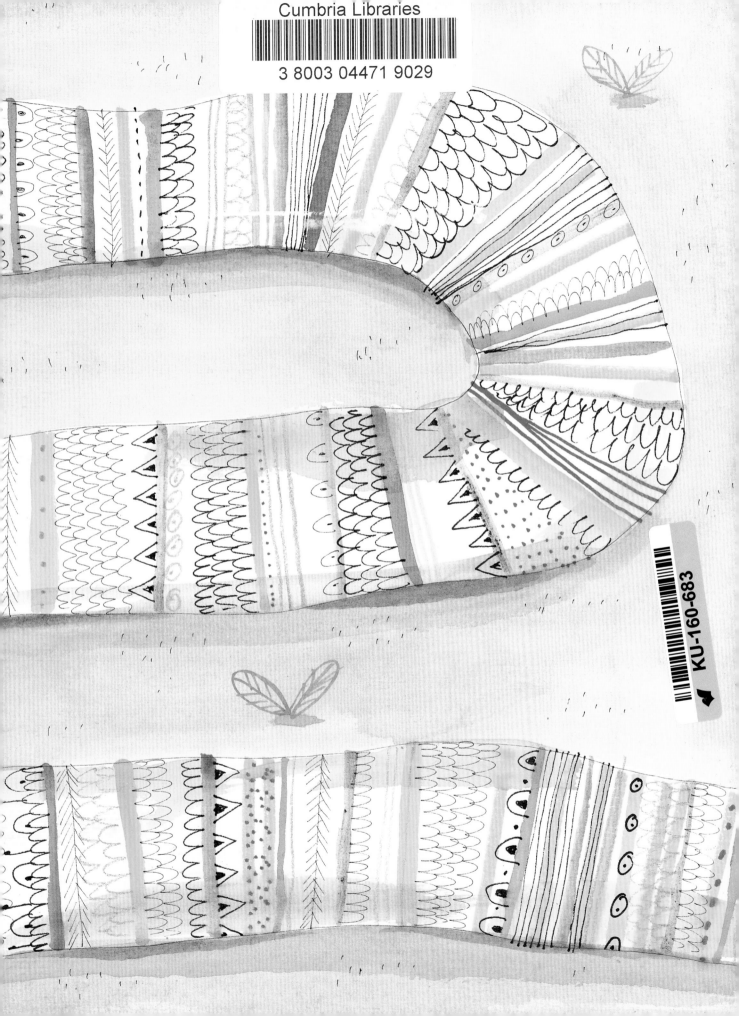

ABOUT THE STORY

There are as many versions of this story in Africa as there are storytellers.
The first written version I know of was one by Edith Rickert
published in 1923, called *The Bojabi Tree*. But it's been retold countless times
and the magical tree has had many names. I've retold the version I know
and love best, changing elements to suit my particular story. It's a story
for children who enjoy nonsense names and rhymes. The repetitive element
helps the idea of the story being a journey.
When I tell it I play an African thumb piano (m'bira)
and use percussion to add to the sense of rhythm.

To Amelia and Jack
and all the pupils at Bertrum House School – DH

for Elise, Alna, Emma and Noëlline – PG

JANETTA OTTER-BARRY BOOKS

The Magic Bojabi Tree copyright © Frances Lincoln Limited 2013
Text copyright © Dianne Hofmeyr 2013
Illustrations copyright © Piet Grobler 2013

First published in Great Britain and in the USA in 2013 by
Frances Lincoln Children's Books, 3 Torriano Mews,
Torriano Avenue, London NW5 2RZ
www.franceslincoln.com

A catalogue record for this book is available from the British Library.

ISBN 978-1-84780-295-8

Illustrated with watercolours

Set in Hoosker Dont

Printed in Shenzhen, Guangdong, China by C&C Offset Printing in January, 2013

1 3 5 7 9 8 6 4 2

The Magic Bojabi Tree

Piet Grobler • Dianne Hofmeyr

F

FRANCES LINCOLN
CHILDREN'S BOOKS

Long ago a dry wind blew across the plains of Africa.
No rain fell. The grass shrivelled. Trees died.
The earth was as dry as a piece of old leather.
Elephant, Giraffe, Zebra, Monkey and Tortoise trudged
across the cracked earth looking for a smidgen to eat.

Then in the distance they saw a tree.
What a marvellous tree it was — covered in
red, ripe fruit smelling of sweetest mangoes,
fat as melons, juicy as pomegranates.

But wrapped tightly around the tree
was the largest python the animals
had ever seen. His coils held the branches
up so high that not even the tallest giraffe
could reach the fruit.

"Leave this to me," said Elephant. "I'm not scared of a python. A python could never swallow me."

He stepped forward. "Excuse me, Python, we're hungry. Please would you uncoil so we can reach the fruit?"

"Not until you've told me the name of the tree."

"That's absurd!" said Elephant.

"We don't know its name."

Tiny Tortoise spoke up. "My great great grandmother told me about this tree. Only the King of the Jungle knows its name, but he lives far away."

"I run faster than all of you," said Zebra. "I'll go."

So Zebra shot off across the hot, dry earth. He ran and ran until he finally came to a cool shelter where the king was lying in the shade, with his mane beautifully fluffed and his tail neatly curled.

"Great King!" said Zebra. "We're hungry. We've found a sweet-mango-melon-pomegranate tree, but Python won't let us eat the fruit until we say the name of the tree."

Lion opened one eye. He didn't like being disturbed when he was snoozing.

"A mango-melon-pomegranate tree? The name of the tree is **Bojabi**."

Then he sighed heavily and went back to sleep.

Zebra put his head down and charged back.
He was so busy thinking about how fast
he was going, he tripped over a root and fell.

"What's the name of the tree?" the animals called out.

"The name of the tree is..." Zebra shook his head as he tried to remember. "The name of the tree is...

is...

BONGANI

But of course he was wrong and Python wouldn't budge.

By now the animals were weak with hunger.
"Someone else will have to ask the king,"
they said.

"Let me go," chittered Monkey. "I'm cleverer
than Zebra. I'll remember the name."

So Monkey scampered over the hot earth and
swung through the dry trees, chitter-chattering,
until he came to where the king was lying in the
shade, with his mane beautifully fluffed and his
tail neatly curled.
"Great King!" said Monkey.
Lion lifted his head and roared, "What now?"
"We're hungry. We've found a sweet-mango-
melon-pomegranate tree but Python
won't let us eat the fruit until..."

"I've already told Zebra. Now I'll tell you.
But don't ask again! The name of the tree is **BO-JA-BI**."

Monkey scampered away chittering and chattering.
  "Clever monkey! Clever me!
  Cleverest monkey in the whole country!"
  He was so busy chitter-chattering that when
he got to the tree he suddenly stopped.

"What's the name of the tree?" the animals groaned.

"The name of the tree is..." Monkey shook his head as he tried to remember. "The name of the tree is... is...

Munjani

But of course he was wrong and Python wouldn't budge.

Elephant pushed himself forward. "I'll go.
Elephants *never* forget."

So he plodded over the hot dry earth.
The king was wide awake by now. His mane was
ruffled and his tail was twitching.

"Great King!" said Elephant. "We're hungry.
We've found...

"I know! And you want to know the name of
the tree. I've told Zebra. I've told Monkey.
And I'll tell you. But I'm **NOT** telling anyone else.
The name of the tree is **BO-JA-BI**! So don't forget!"
Elephant flapped his ears and stamped up some dust.
"I never forget anything!" he said in a huff.

All the way back, he flapped and stamped.
"Hah! Me? Forget? What does a lion know?
I can remember all the rivers in Africa, all the stars
in the sky, all the insects on this earth."
He was so busy remembering them that
when he got to the tree he suddenly stopped.

"What's the name of the tree?"
the animals whispered hoarsely.
"The name of the tree is..."
Elephant shook his head. "The name
of the tree is... is...

UMPANI

But of course he
was wrong and Python
wouldn't budge.

Tiny Tortoise spoke up. "Let me go!"
The other animals laughed at him.
"You're too tiny and slow," they said.
"But I know how to remember,"
said Tortoise. "My great great
grandmother taught me."

So tiny Tortoise crept over the hot dry
earth one slow footstep at a time. When he
eventually reached the king he was pacing up
and down with his mane standing out in angry
tufts and his tail snapping through the air.

Lion took one look at
Tortoise and roared.
**"I KNOW WHAT YOU'VE
COME FOR!** I've told Zebra.
I've told Monkey.
I've told Elephant.
Now **I WON'T** tell you!
I won't tell you the name
of the tree is...

BOJABI!

Tiny Tortoise crept off without saying a word.
"Bojabi," he whispered to himself.

"Bojabi for you. Bojabi for me.
What will bring down the fruit of the tree?
Bojabi! Bojabi! Bojabi!"

All the way back he sang his song.
And because he walked so carefully and slowly,
he didn't stumble, or bump into things, or forget.

"Bojabi for you. Bojabi for me.
What will bring down the fruit of the tree?
Bojabi! Bojabi! Bojabi!"

Bojabi   Bojabi   Bo

The moment Python heard the words he uncoiled
and slithered away. The branches of the tree bent low.
The animals reached up and tasted the red, ripe fruit
that smelled of sweetest mangoes, fat as melons,
juicy as pomegranates.

Mmmm! It was better than anything they had
ever tasted. They ate and ate.

Then the animals lifted tiny Tortoise high.
They circled the tree and sang...

"*Bojabi for you. Bojabi for me.*
We know the name of this magical tree.
BOJABI BOJABI BOJABI

And they never forgot.

Now, do *you* know the name of this magical tree?

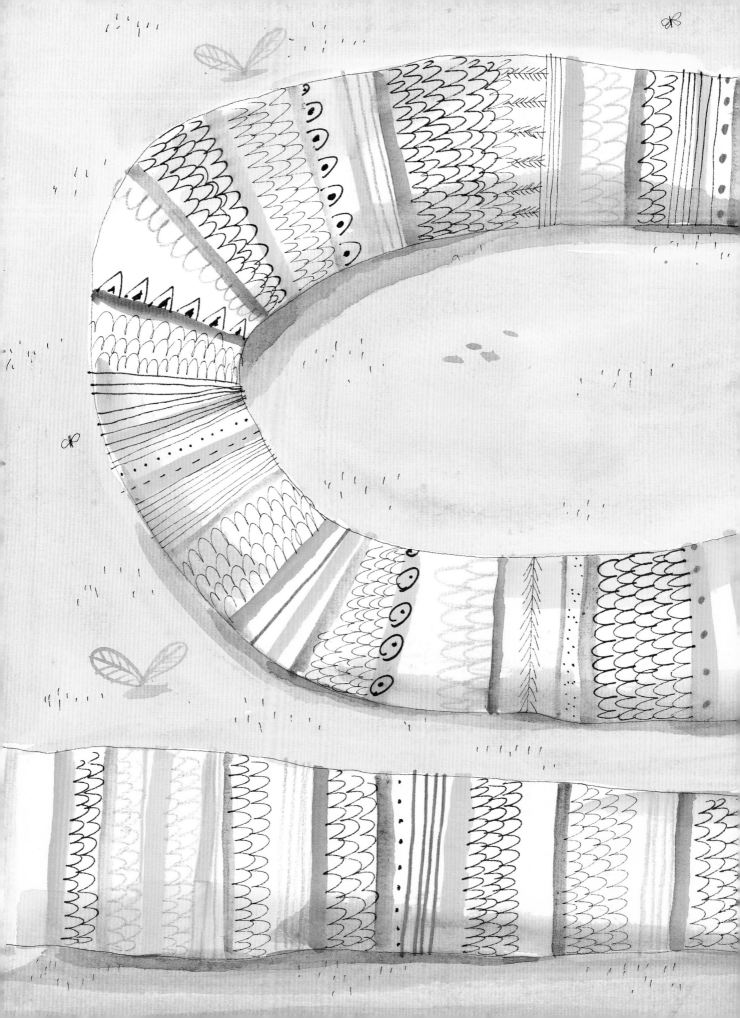